# David and the Trash-Talkin' Giant

*from 1 Samuel 16 &17*

## MR. GRUNGY'S™ ART GALLERY

*Here are the winning entries to Mr. Grungy's nation-wide trash art contest.
These and many other kids have learned how to turn trash into treasure
by being creative and keeping God's earth beautiful!*

*Lion*
*by Jessica Smith, Age 7*
*Birmingham, AL*

*Lamb*
*by Amber Stone, Age 11*
*Garland, TX*

*Heart*
*by Nathan Roush, Age 5*
*Lawrenceville, GA*

Published in Nashville, Tennessee, by Tommy Nelson™, a division of Thomas Nelson, Inc.

**Library of Congress Cataloging-in-Publication Data**
Anderson, Joel.
    David and the trash talkin' giant / by Joel Andeson;
illustrations by Joel Anderson and Abe Goolsby.
      p.  cm.
    At head of title: "Mr. Grungy's seek & find Bible stories."
    Summary: Rhyming text and illustrations present the Bible story of
David and his defeat of the Philistine giant Goliath
      ISBN 0-8499-5918-7
      1. David, King of Israel--Juvenile literature.  2. Goliath (Biblical giant)--Juvenile literature.
    [1. David, King of Israel. 2. Goliath (Biblical giant) 3. Bible stories--O.T.]  I. Goolsby, Abe, ill.  II. Title.
    BS580.D3A57   1999
    222'.4309505--dc21
                                                         98-46163
                                                           CIP
                                                           AC

Printed in the United States of America

99 00 01 02 03 RRD 9 8 7 6 5 4 3 2 1

# David and the Trash-Talkin' Giant

## by Joel Anderson

*Illustrations by Abe Goolsby and Joel Anderson*
Digital photography by William Jackson Goff

**Tommy™ NELSON™**

Thomas Nelson, Inc.

Nashville

To my mom and dad,
Mary and Charles Anderson,
who never thought I was
too small to face giants.
Love, Joel

And (David) took his staff in his hand, and
chose him five smooth stones out of the brook,
and put them in a shepherd's bag which he had...
                    I Samuel 17:40
I chose these 5 stones from the same brook
in Israel in 1994.        Dad

To my wife, Shannon:
Without the joy you bring to me
what a junk-filled
place my life would be!
I love you. Abe

Special thanks to Tony Novak for
his junk scrounging and artistic contribution.

"Mr. Grungy is my junkyard name. My trinkets tell true stories in art.
Most people look at the outside appearance, but God looks at the heart."

Trash & Treasure Hunt

Find eight light bulbs and four keys. Find the postage stamps (there are five of these). Count six paper clips, seventeen peanut shells, and say the word that the bunch of letters spells.

There once was a boy named David, the youngest of eight brothers. His job was to watch the sheep. (A job too small for the others.)

While watching sheep, he would play his harp, and often he would sing.
He was a faithful boy who loved the Lord more than anything.

David was small, but he could pray ... especially when a lion roared!
He once killed a lion and saved his sheep with courage from the Lord.

4

Trash & Treasure Hunt
Find eighteen stars, nine marbles,
six combs for your hair,
part of an old baseball, eight bugs,
and a wasp nest . . . if you dare!

5

There was a prophet named Samuel who obeyed God in everything.
God spoke to Samuel one day and said, "I've chosen the future king."

Trash & Treasure Hunt
Find thirteen candles, nine bottle caps,
eight things which draw or write,
four pennies, and a dinosaur
who is ready to take a bite.

God said, "Go secretly to Bethlehem. Find a man named Jesse there.
One of his sons will be king someday.  Quickly, go prepare!"

God told Samuel, "Don't pick the tallest one. Don't set the strong apart.
Man looks on the outward appearance, but the Lord looks at the heart."

Trash & Treasure Hunt
Find four animals and
eight different things to eat.
Find a spoon and three nails,
and point to something sweet.

The youngest and smallest was David.  God said, "He's the special son.
Someday he'll be the king of Israel, My anointed one."

At that time, Saul was the king. He was often sick and sad.
He wanted someone to play the harp, so he wouldn't feel so bad.

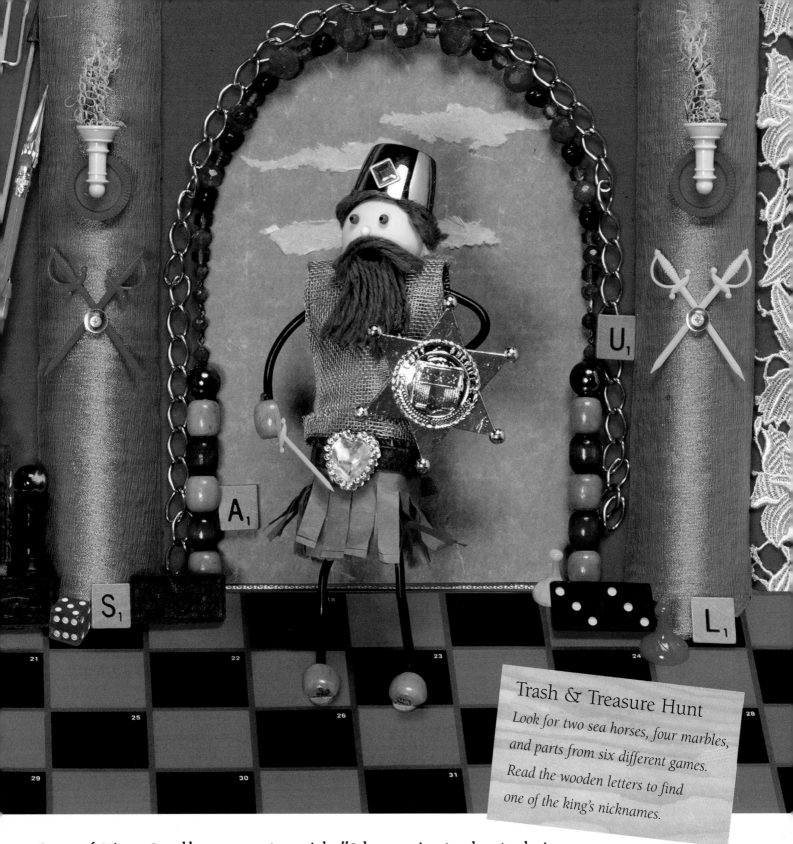

Trash & Treasure Hunt
Look for two sea horses, four marbles, and parts from six different games. Read the wooden letters to find one of the king's nicknames.

One of King Saul's servants said, "I know just who to bring. There is a shepherd boy named David who can play the harp and sing."

The king was very pleased when David came to play.
He started to feel better and grew happier every day.

## Trash & Treasure Hunt

Find five yo-yos, six paper clips,
and six things for your hair.
Spot a fish, a bird, a key, a screw,
and a very sporty chair.

Trash & Treasure Hunt
Find a fish, a goose, a frog,
and eight things that can fly.
Spot a six-pointed star
on a very dressed up guy.

So David got to stay in the palace. He even had a place to sleep.
But he often went back to his father's field to help out with the sheep.

David thought of his anointing. One day he'd be the king!
But for now he was just as happy to watch the sheep and sing.

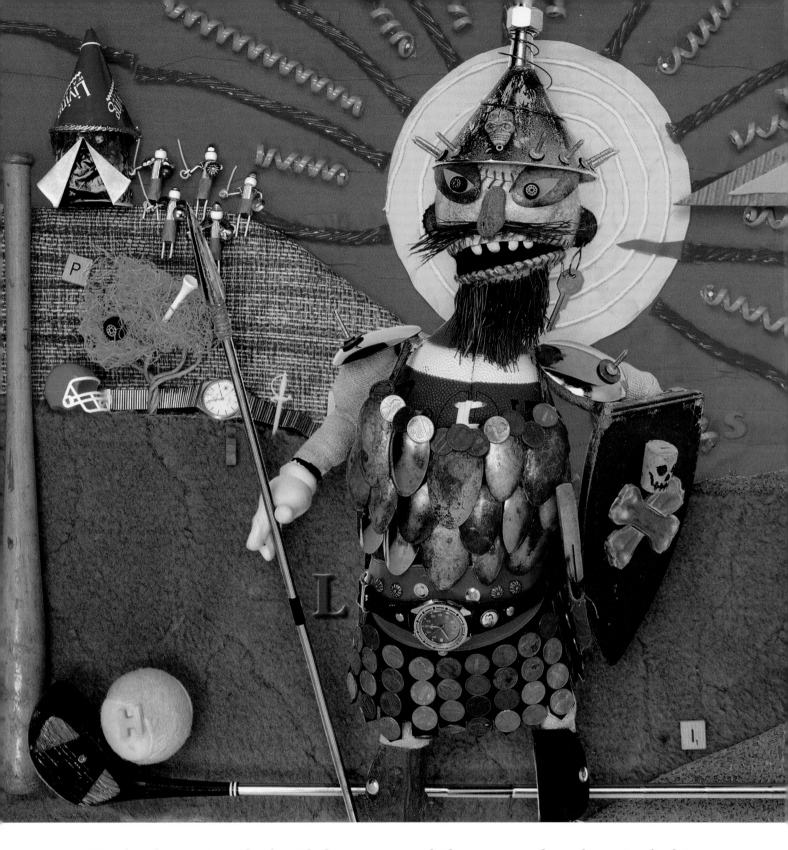

War broke out with the Philistines, and the enemy lined up to fight.
They had a nasty giant soldier who filled everyone with fright.

Trash & Treasure Hunt
Find seven things for sports,
a dart, a bug, and fork.
Find three keys and eight watches.
(It's going to take some work!)

Each day the giant taunted, "Send a man to fight, if you dare!
If you kill me we'll surrender. But if I win, just beware!"

David's brothers were in the army, and he came to bring them food.
David heard the trash-talkin' Giant and thought that he was rude!

Trash & Treasure Hunt
*Find two kinds of bread
and three things which are sweet.
Find the alphabet soup letters
and a cracker someone tried to eat.*

"Who will fight this loud-mouth giant? He's the foulest of mean brutes!"
But no one would come forward. They all stood shaking in their boots.

David said, "I'll fight that giant! With God's help I'll make him fall!"
So the king dressed David in his royal armor, but it didn't fit at all.

Trash & Treasure Hunt
Find ten paper clips, six feathers
eight buttons, and five neck ties.
Spot eight leaves, a push pin,
and a horseshoe on something
that is the wrong size.

David said, "I can't wear this!" And he gave the armor back.
From a stream he chose five stones and plopped them in his sack.

David went bravely to the battlefield with a slingshot in his hand.
The giant mocked him and laughed so hard, he almost couldn't stand.

Trash & Treasure Hunt

Find four roaches, a fork, a wheel,
and things kids should NEVER touch.
Find a bike part, seven saw blades, and
a stinger which would hurt very much.

The giant was talkin' trash as he moved forward to attack.
David prayed a prayer for courage as he reached into his sack.

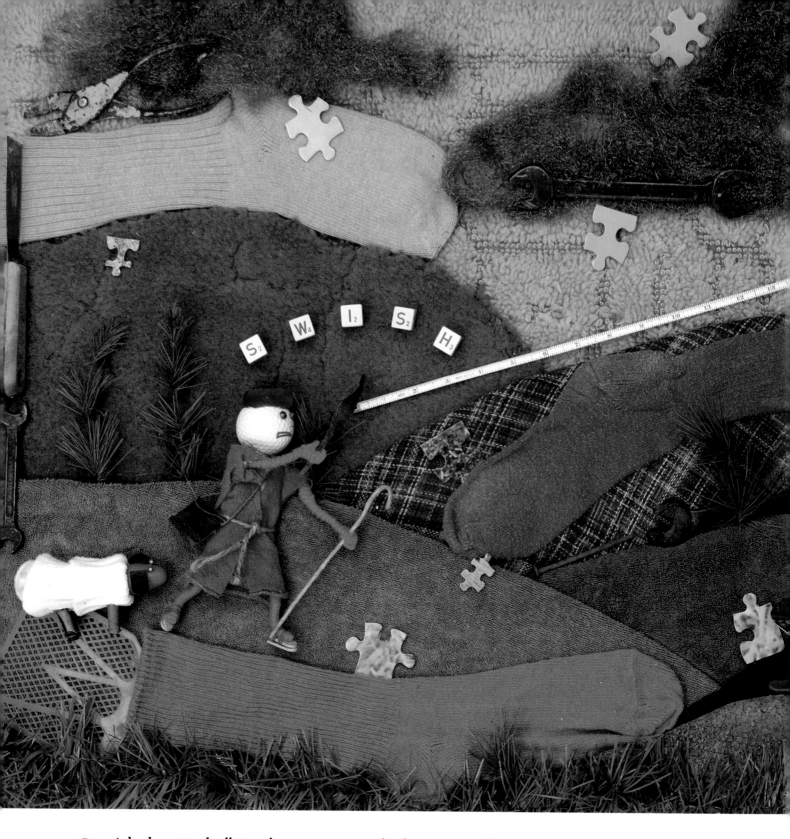

David shouted, "You've come to fight me with your spears and swords!
But today, you'll be defeated because the battle is the Lord's!"

Trash & Treasure Hunt
Find seven tools, fourteen
puzzle pieces, and a word in blue.
Look for four socks, a brush,
and something a dog likes to chew.

He placed a stone inside his sling and slung it 'round and 'round.
He let it fly and it smacked the giant, who tumbled to the ground.

David became very famous, but that was just the start.
Men looked at his outward appearance, but God looked at his heart.

## Trash & Treasure Hunt

*Find a line of coins where one is odd.*
*Spot six bells and a telephone part.*
*Find four pencils and a pair of pears.*
*Point to a lemon and a wooden heart.*

27

Trash & Treasure Hunt
Find a toothbrush, an old king,
the author and his friend.
Find David, the giant, a fork, a key,
and the words that say "The End".

The End